Raffle Ticket No 7
10p
Woodside Dry Cleaners.
receipt for Jacket and bow tie.
Mouse
STAMFORD, LINCS.
Dear Mouse
Weather fine and sunny. Have been Picnicing on common. Love Rat.
Mr. Mouse
The woods
(Just past Rabbits hole)

your sight test is on 7.3.82 at 2.30pm
Mole
you are cordially invited to Rabbits birthday party. Bring a cake. R.S.V.P.
SCUNTHORPE-ON-SEA
Having a lovely time, wish you were here! from Rabbit
To Mole esq.
The Woods
(Near Owls tree)
To be kept
MoLe

For my dear friends —
Nita and Frank Hilton
J. D.

献给我亲爱的朋友妮塔和弗兰克·希尔顿
—— 乔伊斯·邓巴

中英双语

老鼠和鼹鼠

春天的第一朵水仙

[英]乔伊斯·邓巴 著　[英]詹姆斯·梅修 绘　仇春卉 译

中信出版集团 | 北京

图书在版编目（CIP）数据

老鼠和鼹鼠. 春天的第一朵水仙 / (英) 乔伊斯 · 邓巴著 ; (英) 詹姆斯 · 梅修绘 ; 仇春卉译. -- 北京 : 中信出版社, 2021.10（2024. 2重印）
ISBN 978-7-5217-3408-9

Ⅰ. ①老… Ⅱ. ①乔… ②詹… ③仇… Ⅲ. ①儿童故事-图画故事-英国-现代 Ⅳ. ①I561.85

中国版本图书馆CIP数据核字(2021)第151278号

老鼠和鼹鼠 · 春天的第一朵水仙

著　　者：［英］乔伊斯 · 邓巴
绘　　者：［英］詹姆斯 · 梅修
译　　者：仇春卉
出版发行：中信出版集团股份有限公司
　　　　（北京市朝阳区东三环北路27号嘉铭中心　邮编　100020）
承 印 者：北京启航东方印刷有限公司

开　　本：889mm × 1194mm　1/16　　印　　张：3.25　　字　　数：60 千字
版　　次：2021 年 10 月第 1 版　　印　　次：2024 年 2 月第 8 次印刷
京权图字：01-2021-1891
书　　号：ISBN 978-7-5217-3408-9
定　　价：28.00元

出　　品：中信儿童书店
图书策划：如果童书
策划编辑：安虹　　责任编辑：孙婧媛　安虹　　营销编辑：张远　邝青青　张超
封面设计：谢佳静　　内文排版：王莹

目录

水仙花

春意荡漾在空气里。鼹鼠欢快地在院子四处蹦蹦跳跳，嘴里还哼着小曲儿：

花间有蝴蝶，树上有小鸟。

蜜蜂处处飞，春光无限好。

我要开心唱，歌声停不了。

突然，他朝着老鼠大声喊：“快来看！快来看！”

老鼠连忙从屋子里跑出来，看见鼹鼠站在院子里，盯着一朵漂亮的黄色水仙花。

“看！我们院子里有朵水仙花！”鼹鼠说。

“春天的第一朵水仙。”老鼠说。

“我们拿它怎么办？”鼹鼠说。

“不怎么办，”老鼠说，“好好欣赏就行了。”

“可是，我们不能整天站在这里盯着它呀。”鼹鼠说，“会着凉的。”

“不用整天站在这里盯着呀。”老鼠说，“我们可以进屋嘛。”

“这样一来，我们就看不到水仙花了。”鼹鼠说。

“它又不会自己跑了。”老鼠说，“我们可以时不时走出来跟它打个招呼嘛。”

“好吧。”鼹鼠说。

可是鼹鼠进屋没多久就跑出来了。“你好，水仙花！”他说。

然后老鼠也跑了出来。“水仙花，你好！”他说。

“这样赏花太累了！”进进出出三次后，鼹鼠对老鼠说，“一定有容易点儿的法子呀。”

“我们可以待在屋子里，心里想着这朵水仙花。”老鼠说。

“我有个更好的办法。”鼹鼠说，“为什么不把它摘下来呢？”

“把它摘下来的话，它就不在院子里了。”老鼠说。

“可是我们可以把水仙花摆在餐桌上，一边吃饭一边欣赏。”鼹鼠说，“也可以把它放在客厅里，一边坐着一边欣赏；还可以把它摆在卧室里，一边睡觉一边闻着花香。”

“这样做当然可以，”老鼠说，“不过，水仙花在院子里会开得久一点儿。”

鼹鼠回到院子里，绕着水仙花走来走去，跪下来闻闻花香，然后又装作没看见水仙花，最后他还是忍不住伸出爪子，把花儿摘了下来。

然后鼹鼠突然大哭起来。

“老鼠，我还是忍不住把水仙花摘了。”他把花儿带进屋里，说道。

“既然这样，我们就趁着花儿还没凋谢，尽情欣赏吧。”老鼠说。

于是，他们把水仙花摆在餐桌上，一边吃东西一边观赏。可是鼹鼠发现自己什么也吃不下。

他们把水仙花放在客厅里，一边坐着一边欣赏。可是鼹鼠发现自己完全坐不住。

他们把水仙花摆在卧室里，一边睡觉一边闻着花香。可是鼹鼠发现自己根本睡不着。

熬到半夜，鼹鼠终于忍不住说：“老鼠，我要去院子里，把水仙花插回去。这样的话，明天它就能回到从前的样子了。”

“我还是陪你去吧。”老鼠打着哈欠说。

他们就拿着水仙花来到院子里，想把它插回花茎上。

“唉，我们已经尽力了。”老鼠叹息道。

第二天早上，老鼠先醒了。他径直走到院子里，发现那朵水仙花已经枯萎了，在折断的花茎上耷拉着。

“天哪！”老鼠说，“鼹鼠马上就要来了，他肯定会伤心的。”他连忙把水仙花藏在身后。

没想到鼹鼠走到厨房窗外停住了脚步，高兴得手舞足蹈。

“快看！”他向老鼠喊道，“春天的第一朵水仙！我们成功把它插回去啦！它看起来就像刚盛开似的！可是，老鼠啊，这朵水仙花昨天是在那边，今天却到了这里，你不觉得奇怪吗？”

“是有点儿奇怪。”老鼠说。

“我应该把它移回去吗？”

老鼠想了想。“呃……不要。”他喃喃地说，“我看还是不要动了，因为现在我们在屋里屋外都能看见它。我们应该吃顿丰盛的早餐庆祝一下。”

于是，他们吃了一顿丰盛的早餐。

胡子

“不对称！”鼹鼠盯着镜子大声嚷嚷，“不对称！我不对称！”

“你哪里不对称？”老鼠问。

“看看我的胡子！”鼹鼠说，“它们一边长一边短。”

老鼠仔细瞧了瞧。“只是长了一点点罢了。”他说，“没有人会留意的。再说了，这叫不对称美呀。”

“可我更喜欢对称美。”鼹鼠说，“胡子就是对称才美。”

“不对。”老鼠说，“很多东西都不是对称的。看看我的眼睛，虽然都是棕色的，可是一只比另一只颜色更深。还有，我的左耳也比右耳尖一点儿。”

“哼，反正我就是不喜欢不对称。”鼹鼠说，“我要把左边的胡子剪长一点儿，好和右边的对称。老鼠，剪刀在哪里？”

“鼹鼠。”老鼠说。

“什么事？”鼹鼠说。

“你不能把东西剪长，只能把东西剪短。”

“那我就把右边的胡子剪短一点儿，好和左边的对称。”鼹鼠说。

鼹鼠用一把大剪刀将右边的胡子剪短了一点儿，又去照镜子。“我剪得太短了。”他说，“现在左边的胡子比右边长，还得把左边的剪短一点儿。”

于是，鼹鼠把左边的胡子剪短。

可他又不小心剪多了，只能把右边的胡子再剪短一点儿，好和左边的胡子对称。

然而他还是不小心剪多了，只能把左边的胡子再剪短一点儿，好和右边的胡子对称。

到最后，他的胡子还是不对称！

咔嚓！咔嚓！咔嚓！鼹鼠继续把剪刀移到另一侧。咔嚓！咔嚓！咔嚓！

接下来，鼹鼠和老鼠大眼瞪小眼，都说不出话来。

“你都干了些什么呀！”老鼠倒吸了一口气。

“我都干了些什么呢？”鼹鼠也倒吸了一口气。

“你把两边的胡子都剪没了！”老鼠说。

“真的呀！”鼹鼠说着，泪如泉涌，“哎呀！我可怜的胡子啊！”他尖叫起来。

“这也不怪你，它们原本就不对称嘛。”老鼠安慰他。

“可是没有人会留意的呀！”鼹鼠号啕大哭，“短胡子也好，长胡子也好，什么胡子都好，我就要我的胡子呀！”

这时，刺猬上门来，看看到底发生了什么事儿。接着，兔子来了，褐鼠也来了。“鼹鼠怎么了？”他们问道。

“他刚才在修剪胡子。”老鼠说，“没想到一下子剪多了，剪得只剩下胡子茬儿了。”

“胡子茬儿啊！”刺猬说，“哈！我宁愿要胡子茬儿也不想要胡子！哪天也给我剪成胡子茬儿吧！”

“胡子茬儿比胡子好多了！”兔子说，“胡子茬儿不会夹在门缝里。”

“还不会沾上果酱。”褐鼠说。

“你也不用整天花时间去打理。”兔子说。

鼹鼠皱了皱鼻子，又摸一下嘴边的短毛。“这就是你们说的胡子茬儿呀？”他说，“胡子茬儿……我喜欢这叫法。”说着他又拿起了剪刀。“还有谁想要胡子茬儿？”

“呃……待会儿见。”兔子说完，一溜烟跑回家了。

“我有件很重要的事儿要办。”刺猬说。

“糟糕，我忘了关水龙头！”褐鼠说。

大伙儿都走了，老鼠若有所思地看着鼹鼠。“胡子茬儿只有一个缺点，”他说，“如果你放任不管，它们就会长成胡子。”

“是吗？”鼹鼠说。

“那你就能变来变去啦。”老鼠说，“今天是胡子茬儿，明天是胡子。”

“妙极了！”鼹鼠说，“这就两全其美了！”

“我们把地扫干净好吗？”老鼠说。

于是，他们用一把短毛刷子把地上的胡子扫干净了。

最不期待了

老鼠在园子里翻土，鼹鼠在旁边看着。

“老鼠，”鼹鼠说，“不知道为什么，我有个预感，今天会发生一件激动人心的事情。”

“这样一来，这事儿就不会发生了。”老鼠说。

“为什么呢？”鼹鼠说。

“当你期待一件事情发生，它往往不会发生。可在你最不期待的时候，这事儿偏偏就会发生。”

“真的吗？”鼹鼠说。

老鼠点了点头，继续埋头翻土。

“这样看来，”鼹鼠说，“我这一生就是一个大错误。每天我都期待有事情发生，可是每天都落了空。”

“总会有事情发生的，”老鼠说，“只是未必如你所愿罢了。”

“老鼠！”鼹鼠突然变得很兴奋，“要是我们对各种好事完全不期待，它们是不是就可能发生了？”

“这我倒没想过。”老鼠说。

“我们应该最不期待什么呢？”鼹鼠说，“你起的话头，老鼠，你可以先说说。”

“这个嘛……”老鼠抓了抓脑袋，“我最不期待的事情，就是我正在翻的这片土地上，突然长出一棵结满了苹果馅饼的大树。”

于是，老鼠和鼹鼠就等啊等，努力不去想一棵结满苹果馅饼的大树从地里长出来。

他们抬头看看天，吹起了小曲。

他们对着爪子看来看去，还做了一大碗蛋奶沙司。

然后他们盯着那一小块地——他们最不期待的，就是一棵苹果馅饼树从地里长出来。

这棵树始终都没有出现。

“老鼠，你这个‘最不期待’的力度还不够大呀。”鼹鼠说。

“那你来吧。”老鼠说。

鼹鼠想了想，说道：“我最不期待的，就是一个神秘的好心人偷偷给我寄来一个神秘的包裹，上面还绑着漂亮的丝带。”

于是，老鼠和鼹鼠就等啊等，竭力不去想那个神秘好心人寄来的神秘包裹。

他们除了一点儿草。

他们沏了一壶茶。

他们还打了一局乒乓球。

他们从厨房抽屉里翻出一把剪刀，准备用来剪绑包裹的丝带。然后他们跑向门口，看看神秘好心人的神秘包裹送来了没有。

包裹还没到。

“鼹鼠，你这个‘最不期待’的力度还不够大呀。”老鼠说。

“哼！”鼹鼠说，“我才不信你这些‘最不期待’的鬼话呢！根本就没用！不管你有没有期待，都不会有好事发生。我放弃了。”

“我也放弃了。”老鼠说。

就这样，他们瘫倒在壁炉旁的沙发上。

突然响起了敲门声。

“先别开门！”老鼠说。

“为什么？”鼹鼠问。

“想想谁在敲门，你‘最不期待’的是哪位？”

“我‘最不期待’的，应该是我那位好久不见的大伯。”鼹鼠说，“他很有钱，腰缠——”

“我猜是褐鼠来借点儿糖。”老鼠说。

果然是褐鼠，不过他不是来借糖的。只见褐鼠戴着一顶圆锥派对帽，风风火火地冲进门。他身后跟着兔子、刺猬和猫头鹰，大伙儿都戴着派对帽。

“生日快乐，鼹鼠！”他们说完，递给鼹鼠一个巨大的苹果馅饼，还有一个绑着丝带的礼物包裹。

“生日？谁的生日？我的生日？”鼹鼠说。

“老鼠在一个星期前就告诉我们了。”褐鼠说。

“‘最不期待’其实挺难办的。”老鼠说，“不能出半点儿差错。”

“你完全没出差错呀！”鼹鼠说，“我真的完全没有期待。好了，老鼠，那碗蛋奶沙司在哪里？还有，哪位把剪刀递给我？”

“为鼹鼠干杯！”褐鼠举起玻璃杯说。

“为鼹鼠干杯！”大伙儿一起说。

“为我干杯！”鼹鼠轻叹一声，很开心地说。

MOUSE & MOLE
Have a Party

Joyce Dunbar and James Mayhew

Daffodil

Spring was in the air. Mole skipped around the garden, singing to himself.

'O butterfly, O bee,
O bird up in the tree,
What fun it is to be
Springy, singy me.'

Then, 'Come and see! Come and see!' he called to Mouse.

Mouse went rushing outside. There stood Mole, staring at a bright yellow daffodil.

'Look. A daffodil growing in our garden!' said Mole.

'The first daffodil of spring,' said Mouse.

'What shall we do with it?' said Mole.

'We don't have to do anything with it,' said Mouse.

'We just admire it.'

'But we can't stand here all day staring at a daffodil,' said Mole. 'We'll get cold.'

'We don't have to stand here all day staring at a daffodil,' said Mouse. 'We can go indoors.'

'But we won't be able to see the daffodil,' said Mole.

'It will still be here,' said Mouse. 'We can run out every so often and say hello to the daffodil.'

'So we can,' said Mole.

No sooner were they inside the house than Mole rushed out again. 'Hello, daffodil,' he said. Then Mouse rushed out. 'Hello, daffodil,' he said.

'This is very tiring,' said Mole to Mouse, when they had rushed in and out three times. 'There must be an easier way.'

'We could stay indoors and think about the daffodil,' said Mouse.

'I've got a better idea,' said Mole. 'Why don't we pick the daffodil?'

'If we pick the daffodil, it won't be in the garden anymore,' said Mouse.

'But we could put the daffodil on the kitchen table and look at it while we eat,' said Mole. 'We could take the daffodil into the sitting room and look at it while we sit. We could put the daffodil in the bedroom and smell it while we sleep.'

'We could,' said Mouse, 'but the daffodil will last

longer in the garden.'

Mole went outside. He walked around the daffodil. He knelt down and smelt the daffodil. He pretended to ignore the daffodil. Then he put out his paw and picked it.

Next he burst into tears.

'Mouse, I have picked the daffodil,' he said, carrying it indoors.

'Well, we'd better enjoy it all we can,' said Mouse. They put the daffodil on the kitchen table to admire it while they ate, but Mole found that he couldn't eat.

They put the daffodil in the sitting room to look at it while they sat, but Mole found that he couldn't sit.

They put the daffodil in the bedroom to smell it while they slept, but Mole found that he couldn't sleep.

In the middle of the night, Mole said, 'Mouse, I am going out into the garden to stick the daffodil back. Then it will be there in the morning.'

'I'd better come with you,' yawned Mouse.

They carried the daffodil out into the garden and tried to stick it back on its stalk.

'That's the best we can do,' sighed Mouse.

The next morning, Mouse was up first. He went straight outside into the garden. Lying just where they'd left it was a crumpled daffodil with a broken stalk. 'Dear oh dear,' said Mouse. 'Here comes Mole. He will be upset,' and he hid the daffodil behind his back. But Mole had stopped outside the kitchen window. He was dancing with delight.

'Look!' he called to Mouse. 'The first daffodil of spring! We managed to stick it back! It's blooming as good as new! But Mouse, yesterday the daffodil was over there. Today it's over here. Isn't that strange?'

'It is,' said Mouse.

'Shall I move it?'

Mouse thought for a moment. 'Er... no,' he murmured. 'I think not. We can see it now, indoors or out. Let's have a celebration breakfast.'

And they did.

Whiskers

'Lopsided!' said Mole, looking at himself in the mirror. 'Lopsided! That's what I am!'

'Whatsided?' said Mouse.

'Look at my whiskers,' said Mole. 'They are longer on one side than the other.'

Mouse had a careful look. 'Only a teeny bit longer,' he said. 'No-one else will notice. Besides, odd things are nice.'

'Well I like even things better,' said Mole. 'Whiskers are meant to be even.'

'No,' said Mouse. 'Lots of things are odd. Look at my eyes. One is a darker brown than the other. And my left ear is more pointed than my right.'

'Well I don't like being lopsided,' said Mole. 'I'm going to cut my left whiskers longer to match. Where are the scissors, Mouse?'

'Mole,' said Mouse.

'What is it?' said Mole.

'You can't cut things longer. You can only cut them

shorter.'

'Then I shall cut my right whiskers shorter to match,' said Mole.

Mole took a big pair of scissors and snipped his right whiskers shorter. Then he looked at himself in the mirror.

'I have cut them too short,' he said. 'Now my left whiskers are longer than my right whiskers. I shall have to cut those as well.'

So Mole cut his left whiskers shorter to match. But he cut them too short. Then he cut the right whiskers shorter again to match his left whiskers. But he cut them too short. So he cut his left whiskers shorter again to match his right whiskers. And he was still lopsided!

Snip! Snip! Snip! went Mole on one side, then Snip! Snip! Snip! on the other, until there came a moment of terrible silence. Mole looked at Mouse. Mouse looked at Mole.

'What have you done?' gulped Mouse.

'What have I done?' gulped Mole.

'You have clipped all your whiskers right off,' said

Mouse. 'I have,' said Mole, and he burst into floods of tears. 'My poor, poor whiskers,' he wailed.

'But they were a bit lopsided,' said Mouse.

'No-one else would have noticed,' howled Mole. 'Short whiskers. Long whiskers. Any whiskers! Just give me back my whiskers!'

Then Hedgehog came to see what the matter was, followed by Rabbit, followed by Rat. 'What's the matter with Mole?' they said.

'He was trimming his whiskers,' said Mouse. 'But he trimmed them right off. So now he has bristles instead.'

'BRISTLES!' said Hedgehog. 'Oh, I much prefer bristles to whiskers. Give me bristles any day.'

'Much better,' said Rabbit. 'You won't get them trapped in the door.'

'You won't get them sticky with jam,' said Rat.

'You won't have to keep smoothing them down,' said Rabbit.

Mole sniffed and stroked his bristles. 'Is that what you call them?' he said. 'Bristles. I like the sound of bristles.'

He picked up the scissors again. 'Who else would like some bristles?'

'Well, I'll be seeing you,' said Rabbit, running off home.

'I have an important errand,' said Hedgehog.

'I'm sure I left the tap running,' said Rat.

When they had all gone, Mouse looked thoughtfully at Mole. 'There is only one thing wrong with bristles,' he said. 'If you leave them, they grow into whiskers.'

'Do they?' said Mole.

'So you can chop and change,' said Mouse. 'Bristles today, whiskers tomorrow.'

'Wonderful,' said Mole. 'The best of both worlds.'

'Shall we sweep up?' said Mouse.

And they swept up the whiskers with a bristle brush.

Least Expecting

Mouse was digging the garden. Mole was watching.

'Mouse,' said Mole. 'I don't know why, but I have a feeling that something exciting is going to happen today.'

'Then it won't,' said Mouse.

'How's that?' said Mole.

'Things don't happen when you expect them to. Things happen when you least expect them.'

'Is that so?' said Mole.

Mouse nodded and went on digging the garden.

'In that case,' said Mole, 'my whole life has been a mistake. Every day I expect something to happen. Every day it doesn't.'

'Something happens,' said Mouse, 'but not what you expect.'

'Mouse!' said Mole, getting all excited. 'Why don't we least expect all sorts of wonderful things. Then they might happen.'

'I never thought of that,' said Mouse.

'What shall we least expect?' said Mole. 'You start, Mouse. You can have first go.'

'Well,' said Mouse, scratching his head, 'what I least expect is that from this patch of ground I have been digging, a tree will suddenly sprout, laden with apple pies.'

Mole and Mouse waited, trying as hard as they could to least expect an apple pie tree to shoot up from the

ground.

They looked up at the sky. They whistled a little tune.

They examined their paws. They made a large bowl of custard.

Then they looked at the patch of ground where they least expected the apple pie tree to grow. It wasn't there.

'Mouse, you didn't least expect hard enough,' said Mole.

'You have a go,' said Mouse.

After a few moments Mole said, 'What I least expect is that a mystery parcel will suddenly arrive from a secret well-wisher. All done up with string.'

Mole and Mouse waited, trying as hard as they could to least expect the arrival of a mystery parcel from a secret well-wisher.

They did a spot of weeding.

They made a cup of tea.

They played a game of ping-pong.

They searched the kitchen drawers for a pair of scissors to cut string. Then they went running to the door to see if the mystery parcel from a secret well-wisher had arrived.

It hadn't.

'Mole, you didn't least expect hard enough,' said Mouse.

'Bah!' said Mole. 'I don't believe in this least expecting. It doesn't work. Nothing exciting happens whether you expect it or not. I give up.'

'So do I,' said Mouse.

And with that, they slumped down in their fireside chairs.

There was suddenly a knock at the door. 'Don't answer it!' said Mouse.

'Why not?' asked Mole.

'Think who you would least expect it to be.'

'I least expect it to be my long-lost uncle,' said Mole. 'The very rich one, with –'

'And I expect it is Rat, come to borrow some sugar,' said Mouse.

It was Rat, but he hadn't come to borrow some sugar. He was wearing a party hat. In he burst, followed by Rabbit and Hedgehog and Owl, all wearing party hats. 'Happy Birthday, Mole,' they said, handing him a large apple pie and a present done up with string.

'Birthday? Who? Me?' said Mole.

'Mouse told us a week ago,' said Rat.

'It isn't easy to least expect,' said Mouse. 'You have to do it just right.'

'So you do,' said Mole. 'And so we have. Where's that custard, Mouse, and will someone please hand me those scissors?'

'Here's to Mole,' said Rat, raising his glass.

'To Mole,' said everyone else.

'To me,' sighed a very happy Mole.

Raffle Ticket №7
10p
Woodside Dry Cleaners. receipt for Jacket and bow tie.
Mouse
STAMFORD, LINCS.
Dear Mouse,
Weather fine and sunny. Have been Picnicing on common. Love Rat.
Mr. Mouse
The Woods
(Just past Rabbits hole)

OPTICIAN
your sight test is on 7.3.02 at 2.30pm
Mole
you are cordially invited to Rabbits birthday party. Bring a cake. R.S.V.P.
SCUNTHORPE-ON-SEA
Having a lovely time, wish you were here! from Rabbit
To Mole esq.
The Woods (Near Owls tree)
(Don't know Postcode)
MoLe
To be kept
SEAT
7.30
off your